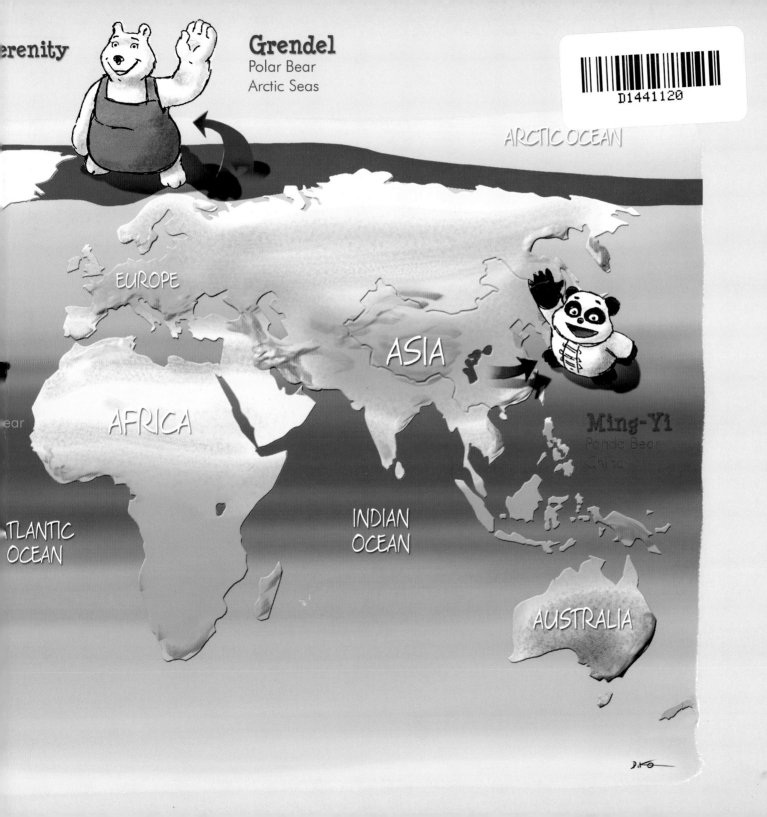

Serenity

Grendel
Polar Bear
Arctic Seas

ARCTIC OCEAN

EUROPE

ASIA

AFRICA

Ming-Yi
Panda Bear
China

INDIAN
OCEAN

ATLANTIC
OCEAN

AUSTRALIA

Fernando and Mackenzie

Serenity

Ming-Yi

Aurora and Ursa Major

Grendel

Remember...
One Small Person
Can Make a Very
Big Difference — That's You!

Enjoy!!

John McQuarey

Bear Hugs!!

The Legend of Honey Hollow

Book One
of the Honey Hollow Series

Written by **Jeanne McNaney**

Illustrated by **David Cochard**

OVATION
Books

Acknowledgments:

To my wonderful friends and family for their unending love, support, and encouragement; to David and Sandrine for their patience and dedication to the project; and to Annie Manlulo for raising awareness about the environmental peril we are now facing on our precious planet.

The Legend of Honey Hollow: Book One of the Honey Hollow Series
Published by Ovation Books in association with Joey Publishing

For more information about our books, please write to us at P.O. Box 80107, Austin, TX 78758, call 512.478.2028, or visit our website at www.ovationbooks.net.

Distributed to the trade by National Book Network, Inc.

Publisher's Cataloging-in-Publication
(Provided by Quality Books, Inc.)

McNaney, Jeanne.
    The legend of Honey Hollow / written by Jeanne McNaney ; illustrated by David Cochard.
    p. cm.
    SUMMARY: The forest of Honey Hollow, once a sanctuary from pollution and destruction, is destroyed by developers, and the bears work together to restore their habitat.
    Audience: Ages 4-8.
    LCCN 2007943685
    ISBN-13: 978-0-9790275-9-8
    ISBN-10: 0-9790275-9-4

    1. Endangered species--Juvenile fiction. 2. Bears--Juvenile fiction. 3. Wildlife conservation--Juvenile fiction. [1. Endangered species--Fiction. 2. Bears--Fiction. 3. Ecology--Fiction.]   I. Cochard, David, ill. II. Title.

PZ7.M232522Leg 2009   [Fic]
                             QBI07-600345

Copyright © 2009 by Jeanne McNaney

Edited by: Maxene Fabe Mulford
Cover and interior design by: Peri Poloni-Gabriel, Knockout Design
www.knockoutbooks.com

Printed on environmentally friendly paper

A percentage of all profits from the sale of this book will go to organizations that support wildlife conservation and endangered species preservation.

For:

Caleigh, Lyndsey, Brendan, and my darling Joe

For the mountains shall depart, and the hills be removed; but my loving kindness shall not depart from thee; neither shall the covenant of my peace be removed, saith the Lord that hath mercy on thee.

–Isaiah 54:10

Winter was ending, and the bears were waking up from their long sleep when a gruff stranger came out of the sea. "Hello? Anybody here?"

Serenity, a brown bear cub, was surprised to see a polar bear so far from its home. "Who are you?" he asked.

"My name is Grendel," she replied, "and I'm very tired because I floated here on a big piece of ice all the way from the Arctic Sea. Is this the famous Honey Hollow where the water is clean, the air is pure, and life is carefree?"

"It sure is!" Serenity answered.

"I came here because humans digging for gas and oil destroyed my home and even killed my best friend. And because of global warming, much of the ice we polar bears live on is melting. When I left my home, my grandcubs were safe, but I'm worried about their future."

"Well, you'll be safe here. C'mon, I'll introduce you to my parents," Serenity said, grabbing hold of Grendel's paw and pulling her along.

"Mom! Dad! Wake up!" Serenity called, bursting into their cave.

"Well, good morning to you too, my son," Aurora answered. "Who's your new friend?"

"This is Grendel, Mom. She had to flee for her life!"

Serenity's father, Ursa Major, was awakened by the noise and asked, "What's the ruckus about?"

Ursa Major was moved after hearing Grendel's story. "You are welcome to stay with us. At Honey Hollow, we take in bears from around the world," he said.

"As the leader of the Bear Council, I want to give you a welcoming gift. This bathing suit is made of special material to protect you from the oil polluting the ocean outside Honey Hollow."

"Thank you very much. I'm so glad that I'm finally safe," Grendel sighed.

Aurora squeezed Grendel's paw comfortingly and then turned to Serenity and suggested, "Why don't you take Grendel outside and introduce her to Mackenzie?"

After the bears went outside, Aurora said to Ursa Major, "I didn't want to say anything in front of Serenity and Grendel, but I'm worried we're in danger too. I'm afraid the men who arrived in trucks last week will cut down our trees. What will happen to all the forest animals? To us?"

Ursa Major bowed his head and shook it sadly from side to side.

Outside, Serenity introduced Grendel to Mackenzie. Grendel was exhausted from her trip and said, "I'm glad to meet you, but I'm too tired to play. I think I'll take a relaxing swim in the river."

"We understand," Serenity and Mackenzie said understandingly.

As Grendel padded off toward the river, the cubs parted ways and happily scampered into the forest.

Mackenzie, a charming black bear cub, once lived in the Appalachian Mountains. But when her bear den was destroyed by coal miners, the bears of Honey Hollow rescued her and brought her back to their home.

While exploring the forest today, Mackenzie found a nest of eggs on the ground. Looking around, she realized she was in her favorite forest grove—but all the trees were gone!

"Oh no!" She picked up the nest and said, "Poor chickies! Something must have happened to your mom. I'd better report this to the Bear Council."

As she made her way to the Bear Council's cave, she saw her friend Fernando, a rare spectacled bear from South America. He was sleeping on a low branch of one of the few remaining trees. Mackenzie nudged him with her elbow.

Fernando woke with a jolt. "¡Qué horror, señorita! ¿Qué pasa?"

Mackenzie showed him the bird's nest and said, "Look what's happened to our forest!"

"O, I know, hija mia," Fernando replied. "I left Peru when the guava trees in my cloud forest were destroyed. I can't believe Honey Hollow's trees are gone now too. Let's find Serenity."

When they found Serenity, he was playing a piano that Ursa Major had carved from a huge mahogany tree. "I hope Grendel hasn't noticed yet that the trees are gone," he said to his friends.

Feeling sad about the changes in their peaceful forest, the three friends bowed their heads in silence.

When they looked up, they saw Grendel relaxing in the river, and they could also see three small humans hiding in the bushes on the far side of the riverbank.

"Uh-oh," Serenity said in a worried voice. "I hope Grendel doesn't notice them. She doesn't like humans, not even children."

While floating in the river, Grendel heard one of the children say, "Look at that bear! Let's try to make her mad enough to chase us. Wouldn't that be fun?"

"What a bunch of little fools!" Grendel thought to herself.

Ignoring the children, she continued resting in the river. She noticed dark thunder clouds in the sky, but because she was from the Arctic, she wasn't bothered by bad weather.

Suddenly, a loud boom of thunder startled the children, and they took off running.

Serenity and his friends were scared too. "Quick! To our cave!" he exclaimed, and they ran through the pouring rain and raging wind.

Inside the cave, their friend Ming-yi, a panda bear from China, was helping Ursa Major and Aurora set cans under leaks to catch the rain dripping from the ceiling.

Ming-yi's name suited him perfectly, since *ming* means "happy" and *yi* means "bright" in Chinese.

Ming-yi arrived in Honey Hollow as a young cub when men in big trucks cleared his bamboo forest home to build their own homes. Frightened and alone, he was rescued by the bears of Honey Hollow and has been happy and grateful ever since.

Today, inside the cave of the Bear Council, Ming-yi cheerfully did his chore. When he saw his three friends, he said, "Nee hau! Why the long faces? Come join us. We're having fun catching rainwater!"

"I wish we could," said Fernando, "but we've got something even more important to tend to."

"The trees are gone!" Serenity said to his mother. "And Mackenzie found this nest lying on the ground. The mama bird must have been killed."

"Then we should care for the eggs until they hatch," Aurora said.

25

"What if my bamboo is also gone!" Ming-yi exclaimed, suddenly leaping to his feet. "I won't have anything to eat!" he said as he rushed outside.

Ursa Major ran after him. "Ming-yi, please wait until the weather eases up!"

Ming-yi looked back and said, "But I've got to check my bamboo...you understand, don't you?"

Ursa Major quietly nodded his head, and Ming-yi took off running.

Ming-yi was stunned by the flooding the storm had caused. With the trees gone, there were no roots left to absorb the water as it poured down the hills.

Suddenly, Ming-yi heard the children shouting, "Help! Somebody save us!" They were being swept away by the strong currents in the river.

"Oh no!" Ming-yi exclaimed helplessly. Then he saw Grendel paddling back from her swim. "Grendel! Quick! Save them!"

Grendel recognized the three children who had tried to tease her earlier, and she turned away, refusing to help.

"Grendel!" Ming-yi exclaimed. "At Honey Hollow, we help each other. Though their parents have damaged our habitat, children are the planet's future. Please rescue them."

Grendel realized that Ming-yi was right, so she swam as fast as she could to a floating tree trunk and gently pushed it toward the children. "Hold on tight," she said.

The children quieted down as Grendel pulled them to the shore.
Once they were safe, she swam back to Honey Hollow.

The next day, the Bear Council met with all the bears of Honey Hollow. The three children Grendel rescued quietly observed from the window.

Ursa Major said, "We're saddened by what happened to our trees. Many of our forest friends died because they couldn't find shelter from the storm. Humans don't realize that cutting down trees hurts the whole forest community. It's harder to find food, and even the air is dirty. What will we do?" Ursa Major asked.

"I will start by planting new trees in the forest," Ming-yi answered. "Who will join me?"

Serenity, Mackenzie, and Fernando stood up and said, "We will!"

"I saw a shovel outside," Grendel added. "I'll get it so we can start now."

When Grendel stepped outside, one of the three children darted over and gave her a big hug. "Oh, white bear! Thank you for saving us in the flood."

This made Grendel happy, and she hugged him back. "Come, little boy, help us save the forest."

"I will, and I'm going to start by asking my dad to stop his men from cutting down trees!" As he started walking home with his friends, he called over his shoulder, "We'll be back to help rebuild the forest."

Several months later, on the first day of spring, birds were chirping, and the seedlings the bears and the children had planted were growing branches. The nest of eggs the bears found the day of the storm rested safely on one nearby. Serenity played his piano while the bears relaxed, enjoying springtime.

Suddenly, Fernando noticed the eggs shaking.

"¡Ayayay! ¡Amigos, it's time!"

The bears gathered around and watched the eggs crack open as little bird beaks pushed through. The chicks were cold because they had no mother to warm them under her wing.

"We'll take turns using our furry paws to keep you warm," Ming-yi said to the baby birds.

A short time later, when the chicks were bigger and ready to be on their own, all the bears gathered for a ceremony. "Little birdies, always remember us," Serenity whispered, gently holding one of the birds.

"We pledge to always care for this forest," Mackenzie said. "Please fly over us once in a while to remind us of this promise."

Then the cubs gave each bird a kiss and set them free.

Over the years, the forest grew thick with trees again, thanks to the Bear Council's care. Now, everyone who visits feels that Honey Hollow is a special place where everyone looks out for one another and gives their environment the love and care it truly deserves.

And each spring, the birds return and fly overhead to remind everyone that children are the planet's future.

SAVE THE ANIMALS...SAVE THE EARTH

Honey Hollow is not a place known to man, but to the bears of the world it is a legend.

The natural environment is rapidly changing, and the global search for energy in the form of oil, gas, and coal is reducing the wilderness necessary for the survival of many animals, including bears.

Fortunately, many distressed bears have found their way to Honey Hollow and can live and prosper in a safe environment. How the bears find their way to Honey Hollow is a mystery. Unfortunately, the reason the bears go to Honey Hollow is understood all too well.

POLAR BEARS ENDANGERED IN THE ARCTIC

Global warming, which threatens to melt away their natural habitat, is only one area of concern for the world's polar bears. The ongoing search for oil and natural gas in the Arctic also greatly reduces their habitat. The encroachment on the polar bear's living space by oil and gas developers also increases the likelihood of accidental oil spills, putting the polar bear at additional risk. Also, many of the fish that polar bears eat live in contaminated waters. Such toxic agents in the food chain are another threat.

BLACK BEARS ENDANGERED IN APPALACHIA

In their search for coal, mining companies first strip away the trees from the mountain habitats of the Appalachian black bear and then blast into mountaintops with explosives. They then dump the remaining blasted rock into the valleys below, polluting streams and poisoning the drinking supply of the black bear. All life forms that live in Appalachia are affected by mountaintop removal, including children and their families.

SPECTACLED BEARS ENDANGERED IN THE ANDES

When farmers in Ecuador, Peru, and northern Bolivia expand the amount of land on which they grow their crops, they greatly reduce the range of the spectacled bear. Pesticides used for farming are another threat. The search for fresh sources of lumber and minerals in the mountain forests is further reducing the natural habitat of this endangered species.

GIANT PANDAS ENDANGERED IN CHINA

More than half of the bamboo forests inhabited by the giant panda have disappeared in recent years. Since bamboo is the mainstay of the panda's diet, it is becoming increasingly difficult for the panda to survive. Fortunately, the children of China have helped raise awareness of the panda's plight. The Chinese are now providing protected bamboo forests that will hopefully save these bears.

Jeanne McNaney lives in Connecticut with her husband, Joseph, and their three children. She is dedicated to causes that enhance the lives of children and their families worldwide. She has degrees in behavioral science and veterinary technology and studied at the Institute of Children's Literature.

French illustrator **David Cochard** has been a freelance illustrator since 1996. After receiving an MA at the University of Paris VIII in 1993, he pursued teaching and later became the chief designer of *Le Goinfre*, an award-winning comic fanzine. Currently residing in Argentina with his wife, Sandrine, he runs his own illustration company, Ilustra World. For more information, please visit:

http://deko.apshram.net/illustraworld

Joey Publishing is a dynamic and growing publisher that produces quality books for young readers that focus on timely issues in the world today. Our wish is to educate children, our world's most precious resource, on important issues and to inspire them to be the best little people they can be as they grow into responsible stewards of God's kingdom. For more information, please visit:

www.joeypublishing.com

Fernando and Mackenzie

Serenity

Ming-Yi

Aurora and Ursa Major

Grendel

The Bears of

Honey Hollow

Ursa Major, Auro
Brown Bears
North America

NORTH
AMERICA

PACIFIC
OCEAN

Macken
Appalachian
Appalachia

SOUTH
AMERICA

Fernando
Spectacled Bear
Andes Mountains